RIBBIT RIDDLES

by **Katy Hall** and **Lisa Eisenberg**

pictures by **Robert Bender**

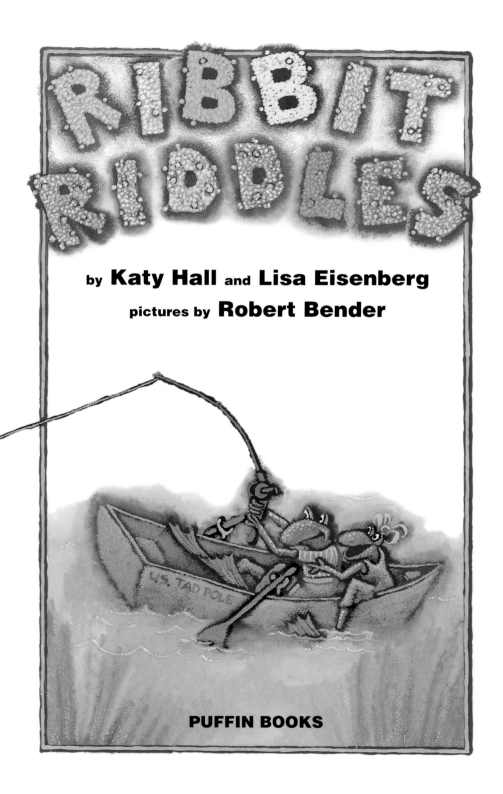

PUFFIN BOOKS

PUFFIN BOOKS
Published by Penguin Group
Penguin Young Readers Group,
345 Hudson Street, New York, New York 10014, U.S.A.
Penguin Books Ltd, 80 Strand, London WC2R ORL, England
Penguin Books Australia Ltd, 250 Camberwell Road, Camberwell, Victoria 3124, Australia
Penguin Books Canada Ltd, 10 Alcorn Avenue, Toronto, Ontario, Canada M4V 3B2
Penguin Books (N.Z.) Ltd, 182-190 Wairau Road, Auckland 10, New Zealand

First published in the United States of America by Dial Books for Young Readers,
a division of Penguin Putnam Inc., 2001
Published by Puffin Books, a division of Penguin Young Readers Group, 2004

1 3 5 7 9 10 8 6 4 2

THE LIBRARY OF CONGRESS HAS CATALOGED THE DIAL BOOKS EDITION AS FOLLOWS:
Hall, Katy.
Ribbit riddles / by Katy Hall and Lisa Eisenberg; pictures by Robert Bender.
p. cm.
Summary: A collection of riddles and jokes about frogs.
Example: What do little frogs like to eat on a hot summer day? Hopsicles!
ISBN: 0-8037-2525-6 (hc)
1. Riddles, Juvenile. 2. Frogs—Juvenile humor.
[1. Riddles. 2. Jokes. 3. Frogs—Wit and humor.]
I. Eisenberg, Lisa. II. Bender, Robert, ill. III. Title.
PN6371.5.H3482 2001 818'.5402—dc21 99-08917

The art for this book was created using cell-vinyl paint on layers of acetate.

Puffin Books ISBN 0-14-240056-4
Puffin® and Easy-to-Read® are registered trademarks of Penguin Group (USA) Inc.

Printed in China

Reading level 2.5

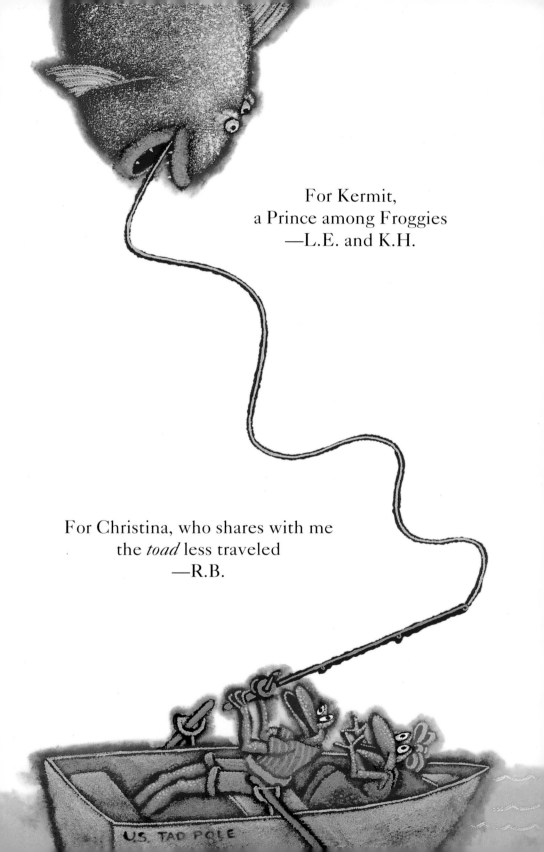

For Kermit,
a Prince among Froggies
—L.E. and K.H.

For Christina, who shares with me
the *toad* less traveled
—R.B.

U.S. TAD POLE

What do little frogs like to eat
on a hot summer day?

Hopsicles!

What happened when the
frog left his car in the
No Parking zone?

His car was toad!

Which froggy was king of
rock 'n' roll?

Elvis Presleap!

What's mean and green and
picks on little tadpoles?

A bully-frog!

What happened when the
Frog Prince married the Frog
Princess?

They lived hoppily ever after!

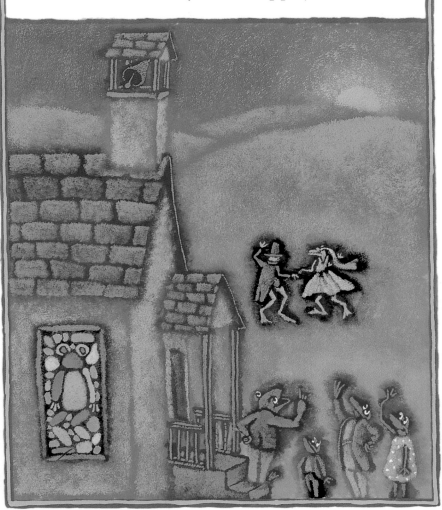

Who brings baskets of eggs to little frogs in the spring?

The Easter Ribbit!

What did one tadpole say to
the other?

"Water you doing?"

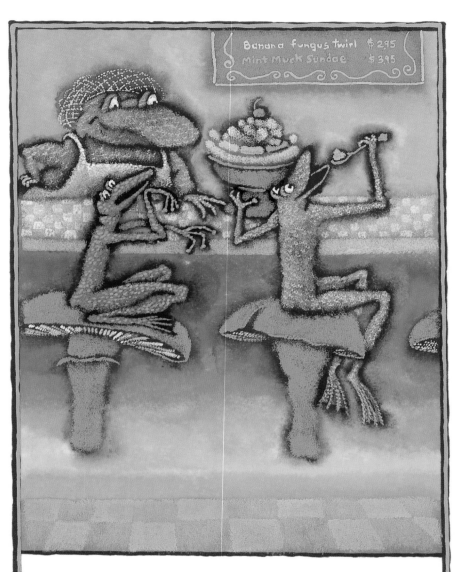

Where do frogs like to sit
at the ice cream parlor?

On toadstools!

Why do frogs make such great baseball players?

They are good at catching flies!

What do frogs like to eat for breakfast?

Hop-Tarts!

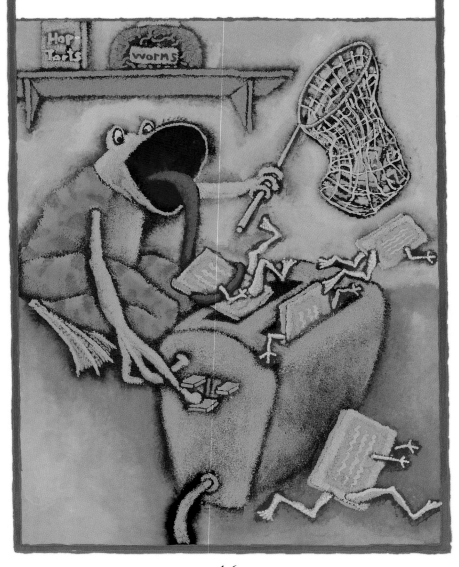

Which ballet is the froggy favorite?

Swamp Lake!

What did the frog ask for
at the fast-food restaurant?

A quarter-ponder and an order of flies!

What do little froggies play
house with?

Dollywogs!

How did the frog look in his
new outfit?

Toadally cool!

What do you call a bunch of froggy footprints?

A website!

Why did the frog say "Tweet"?

She was speaking a foreign tongue!

What did the foot doctor tell
the frog?

"You need a hop-eration!"

Why should you never take a
check from a frog?

It might bounce!

What do froggies drink with their pizza?

Croak!

What do you call a tadpole's hairpiece?

A pollywig!

What do you call froggy sandals?

Open-toad shoes!

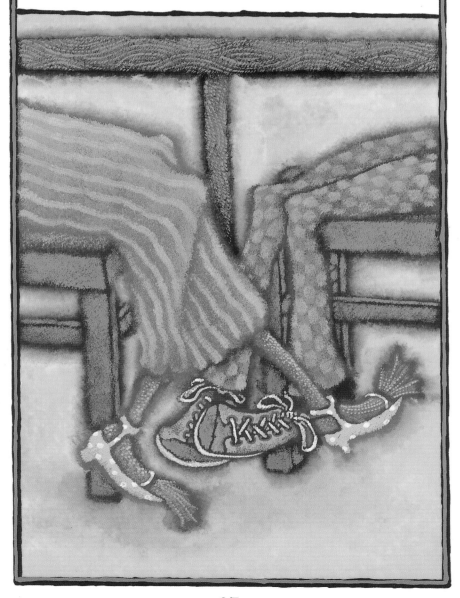

How does a froggy steer a canoe?

With a lily pad-dle!

Why didn't the frog like the trout?

There was something fishy about him!

What game do little frogs play at recess?

Leap people!

What did one toad say to the other toad?

"Wart's up?"

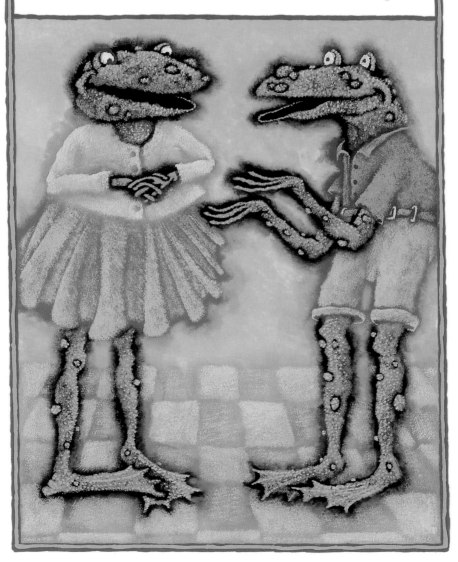

What did the cowboy frogs eat
at the big barbecue?

Spare ribbits!

What goes dot-dot-dot-croak?

Morse toad!

What do you get if you cross a pig with a frog?

A ham-phibian!

Which froggy won the Olympic gold medal?

The tadpole-vaulter!

What's green and tough and
guards the house?

A watch-frog!

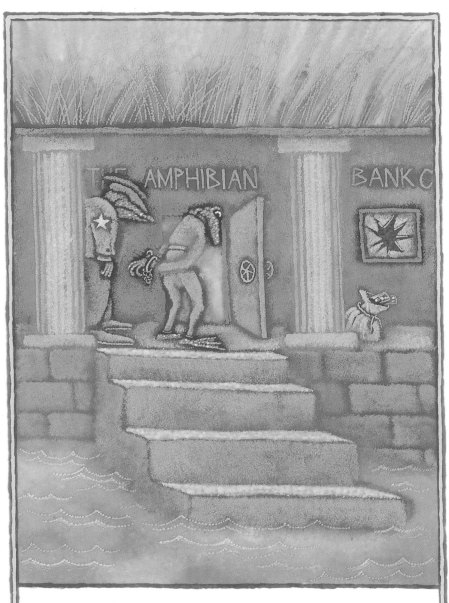

Why did the frog go to jail?

For robbing the riverbank!

What do you get if you cross a
tadpole and a parrot?

An animal that says "Pollywog a cracker!"